The GAME *of* STATUES

The GAME *of* STATUES

Martha Hollander

THE ATLANTIC MONTHLY PRESS
NEW YORK
♦

Acknowledgment is gratefully given to the following magazines, in which some of the poems in this book originally appeared, some in slightly different forms:

Connecticut Artists: "Black Bodies," "'Sur le Pont d'Avignon'"; *Grand Street:* "The Soccer Game outside Munich"; *The Hudson Review:* "Venetian Blinds"; *Operative:* "On Location, with Vampires"; *The Paris Review:* "Difficult Movie"; *Partisan Review:* "Ogata Kōrin on His Field of Irises"; *The Quarterly:* "The Detective Examines the Body"; *Shenandoah:* "Agalma," "The Auto-Architect," "Back in the Twilight Zone," "The Candid Shot," and "Telling Tales"; *Some Other Magazine:* "From an Old Dialogue"; *The Southwest Review:* "Accidents"; *The Yale Review:* "Central Park" and "Pillar of Salt."

"You Are Here," "Views of the Studio," "The Wanderer's Journal," "From an Old Dialogue," "Magnificat," "On Location, with Vampires," "Friend Fever," "Last Seen in Jerusalem," "Sunburn," and "Via Faenza" were published as *Always History,* Sea Cliff Press, 1985.

Published simultaneously in Canada
Printed in the United States of America

Library of Congress Cataloging-in-Publication Data
Hollander, Martha.
    The game of statues / Martha Hollander.
    ISBN 0-87113-369-5 (hc)
    ISBN 0-87113-370-9 (pbk.)
    I. Title.
    PS3558.034945G36   1990   811'.54—dc20   89-28958

Design by Laura Hough

The Atlantic Monthly Press
19 Union Square West
New York, NY 10003

FIRST PRINTING

Winner of the Walt Whitman Award for 1989

Sponsored by the American Academy of Poets,
the Walt Whitman Award is given annually
to the winner of an open competition among American poets
who have not published a first book of poems.

Judge for 1989: *W. S. Merwin*

Contents

The Game of Statues *1*

Venetian Blinds *3*

When We Ride Off *5*

From an Old Dialogue *8*

The Archaeologist's Dream *10*

Friend Fever *13*

Black Bodies *15*

On Location, with Vampires *17*

The Detective Examines the Body *19*

Virgin in the South *25*

Last Seen in Jerusalem *27*

"Sur le Pont d'Avignon" *29*

Incognito *31*

Accidents *32*

Telling Tales *35*

Pillar of Salt *38*

Central Park *40*

You, Me and the Thing *41*

The Silhouette *43*

Views of the Studio *46*

Ogata Kōrin on His Field of Irises *48*

The Candid Shot *53*

The Auto-Architect *55*

Magnificat *57*

Agalma *60*

Back in the Twilight Zone *65*

You Are Here *68*

The Wanderer's Journal *70*

The Soccer Game outside Munich *72*

Via Faenza *74*

The Mourner *77*

Route 280 *79*

Difficult Movie *81*

Sunburn *83*

In the Museum *85*

The Game of Statues

The two small girls playing the game of statues
by the riverbank in Bruegel's universe
hunker down happily in the grass, served up
on the platters of their spread skirts. The third,
who is It, has told them to stop spinning and then
freeze into a recognizable something—
fairy-tale dragon, household artifact—
but how to will yourself into will-lessness?
How to look like anything at all
after being flung around by a friend?
Tucking up their feet, the girls become
lily pads, or muffins topped with cherries,
round and snug, reveling in the exactness
of being so reduced.

                         Their smaller sister
in the snow of Bethlehem flings out her arms
at a frozen pond, stunned into exclamation
by the circling birds above her, by the smooth
yellowish ice glowing with information.
No one touches her. The enormous earth

spins her into action and holds her there
with one command, like the old upheaval
that hurled the people of Herculaneum
into graceful oblivion. Sealed in their own
attitudes of panic, they resemble
nothing, they are nothing but what they were.

In the bath, steam rises calmly from your arm.
You might be drying into something dense
and immovable, encased in the hard limits
offered by silence and surfaces. No wonder
another person's skin will always feel
softer than yours. The world lurches and tilts
with contrasts, with the noise of apprehension
as it turns you loose again, and again you turn
back into what you were: one of them,
poised and ready for the coming round.

Venetian Blinds

On my window I have the new model,
the subtle modern kind: a little twist
of the plastic rod, stiff with crystalline
newness, will always show day to the night.

Surprise—morning already, and all the
heavy light sifts into my room now, breathed
by the glistening landscape of water-
towers and roofs. Summer, city, those two
hot conditions that work the quick changes
on each other, melt and shimmer for hours.
It isn't Venice out there at all whose
buildings wink and crumble like old jewels,
but another rich place framed in brackish
sick sea, when the sun, still echoing stripes
across my late bed, glares over Manhattan.

And it isn't a blond brocaded queen
whose white body is bisected by the
whiter blinds—look, here is a glimpse of breast,

there, the finer curves are compelled into
anonymous shadows. It isn't Titian
approaching the royal nymph to paint her
but a shabby man who sketches, a friend

who looks up now from the burning gray street
as the New York girl, Renaissance-naked,
stands half-hidden at the window and waits.

When We Ride Off

Beginning as usual in the dark
well of an expensive late-night taxi,
you recall this scene: your father rushes
indoors where you, at fifteen, study Greek,
and shouts about the new car. You quit Act
Three of the tragedy, smile, and remove

your glasses; he lets you drive. To remove
myself from that important moment, dark
with suburban closeness, roofs, trees, I act
as if I've always lived in a taxi,
a raw city child, reared above a Greek
restaurant, watching the crowd that rushes

onward past the door just as it rushes
now, in the gloom, always at one remove
from those quiet home roads, those texts in Greek.
You've asked why: because here when it gets dark
the wet streets reflect passion. Our taxi
expands silently for us like an act

of love renewed by the heat of speed. Act
quickly, embrace me as evening rushes
headlong into night like clever taxi
drivers cutting through traffic. I'll remove
only my gloves. In the sibilant dark
we both glimpse our driver's name, which is Greek.

The drive will be like foreign trips, where Greek
temples loom up and come alive to act
as rare, fearful road signs, studding the dark
expanse of Europe. There, forest rushes
to meet citadel, and calm fields remove
the noisy past, monstrous as a taxi

in Arcadia. And our lost taxi
whips through grass, unnoticed, like words in Greek
I forget, like your childhood. You remove
your hand, for in the country we must act

like creatures of earth, wet weeds and rushes,
and knowing where we are, breathe in the dark.

It's dark and resonant as a Greek
theater in the taxi. On it rushes,
removing us from the world in one act.

From an Old Dialogue

The Greek poet, licking a lone
finger to smooth an eyebrow, said:
"Fate is the hand that separates
us, cleaving between with all the
force of tempests." He lived among
brilliant cities of the present,
where the streets gleam more clearly
than any god's flame—languid voice
breaking, head turning for a quick
glance at the receding profile
of a young loved one. Someone had
just left the parlor quietly.

Now I asked him: "Then what binds us?
This fate is our only mother,
the arm bending all around us
to ease the tender quantity
of infant two into grown one.
She scatters our astonishment
from her hand." But I saw his eyes
buried like layers of kingdoms,

gone down below to early things,

and saw that no answer slept there.

This pale Alexandrian, prim

and sickly in my photograph

of him, speaks more faintly now through

the tarnish of afterlife, dim

and brittle city of critics,

of followers, and of lovers.

The power of once errant lips,

eyes, fingers, and wits trembles

inside his lost face. And I remember

hearing of his own probings through

fate's loom and sharp, knotted spindle.

Past all the wet midnight streets and

limestone palaces where he strolled,

lusted, and considered the shape

of the delicious past, I still

find him ironic and mournful,

wasted by weak autumnal fires,

the poet in his silk cravat.

The Archaeologist's Dream

Pain, like a diamond,

can slice through anything,

has a thousand sharp aspects.

I'm a boy of seven again, running,

falling headlong on smooth concrete

and breaking a tooth. I can see

the alien white piece lying there

like bone china destroyed in a rage,

now part of the world's random scatterings.

Stunned by this new absence, I don't even

examine or preserve the brittle bit

the way a sick person coos over

his sore extremities. Instead

I leave it to be lost

in a confusion of children,

trampled and driven underfoot

by decades of small sturdy shoes.

Teeth are the proudest of our ornaments.

It was a front one that broke, and so

history can be read in the small flaw

just as I can read it in pottery sherds,

in the grave, chipped faces of statues.

Teeth urge us to bite as we kiss.
It's many years later, and I am kissed,
it appears, by a woman who eagerly
grasps the nature of artifacts.
She knows something is missing
as she digs in my mouth with her own.
I know she is hunting for that fragment,
for what I'd buried so much earlier,
and her breathless excavation will
bring her what she wants.
My own work on a distant hill unearthed
a few black pebbles, elegantly concave,
that turned out to be ancient garlic.
I bit one, more a challenge than a joke,
and the resonance of the old break
suddenly soared along my jaw. It was
as if that equivocal little rock
would absorb me into its impossible age.
I can feel it now as she hits,
like a pulsing nerve of gold, pay dirt.
She cradles the fragment in the hot
intelligence of her hands, holds it

up to the light, dusts it off,

and laughs aloud at the discovery.

And again the great negative space

invades who I am, shattering my face

into a thousand sharp aspects,

slicing through all of me,

like a diamond, pain.

Friend Fever

The wind of illness blows in her chamber
of its own accord, a pale origin
near both floor and molding. She is doll-eyed,
heavy with disorders that stiffen skin—
and the head closes when the body is
wronged by the weight of another,
in bed with fever, the old companion.

"My dearest, it's the good and bad creatures
fighting inside you." And her brow accepts
a cool big hand, a bit of love whispered
in the left ear, the one huddled in heat.
Ah, but leave her alone now, or almost:
infection creeps in again by her side
and on top of her, shuddering in bliss.

The incubus of sickness lays her out
flat and breathless, sets the immensity
of death in her, hums and batters,
threatens and promises those closer embraces.

She will turn and turn in the useless sheets,

locked in the arms of her ally, body

a ravaged isle of things quivering and

still living—and she is spent, and a bit

of something is whispered to her, that which

feels out of place now but might become love.

Black Bodies

"And oh," says one child, "look at it!
The moon, like a spoon." And of course
in the telescope it's soundless
and friendly, perfect as a roof
of closeness itself. Perhaps it
could fit in her mouth. Whether a
window on the unbearable
brilliance of elsewhere (other skies
behind this one) or a tilted
face thrust among us, or even
the blank heart of our own lone eye,
it just imitates its pictures.
But look—its wavering edges
remind us that it's huge, dead
and buried in the lens, for it
gives itself away with movement.

The children run around the lawn.
As the light dims and thickens, each
moment of daylight awareness
clouds, hesitates, and then freezes;

they become bolder and blinder
in their running. Withdrawn into
the glory of their own skins (just
shells around the soft weighty hulk,
robbed of light, which is a body),
they escape in night. They stamp, shout
and pound sightlessly at the ground,
stopping only when a glimpse of
the great telescope, there outdoors,
makes them remember, holds their moon.

Then the children play warrior.
In the midst of a dramatic
death, when stones, stars and trees hover
with the spin of her flung-back head,
the little girl recalls the round
image she saw. She sighs, wriggles
with delight, and shocks the others
who cry "But you're dead!" for she
gives herself away with movement.

On Location, with Vampires

Here is the absolute horror movie:
the available light never changes.
Here are the tea shops, swiftly boarded up
to look timeless; here is the alley where
the elegant monster sped in silence,
wearing a cloak the color of midnight
after it rains. It has rained ever since.
Deep inside the old cathedral, there are
cameramen scaling the earth-dark stairs
with their tripods nestled against their necks
like stiff familiars. You can see them
crawl and crawl toward each steep parapet,
over the gabled roofs, past unopened
gates and windows, to take the perfect shot
as everything they focus on turns gray.
From this angle the cloaked figure below
has shrunk to a fly gleaming with evil;
now he inches away from this quaint place,
for it grows too weary of his attack
and is sucked dry of its native twilight
that hummed with gnats and drunkards. Now evening
stains the sky with a colder emulsion.

At the first fade to black, this infested
tower begins to shudder, while the town,
bathed in a glossy fever of film, dies
with one peal of its legendary bell.

The Detective Examines the Body

Nothing but an assemblage
of cylinders, it rests
on the sidewalk at dawn.
He sees it easily enough
as the crowd parts,
giving him shy looks
and shuffling back as if
unveiling a monument.
Only a few minutes later
the police come by
to draw a white outline
around the important corpse
before spiriting it away.
Still, the world that is
or was the person
shimmers uneasily at him,
in the blank frame
that waves at nothing
(one arm up, one leg bent)
like an exuberant bit
of graffiti. Stenciled

on the damp ground,

it's as pure and inviting

as a footprint: he's

ready to hurl himself

into the mold

and test the fit.

But there's work to do

among those living

organisms called suspects.

With each visit he returns

to the body's volumes

and superb angles, bones

darting forward, skin and fat

swimming sexily over them.

Calibrated to arouse

and astound, to inspire,

to warn, the real thing

hums with life and language:

hip and shoulder, waist

allied with knee, strike
the room's four walls
like an epiphany. Each
possession there becomes
an extra limb, a bright
icon of motive saluting
his eye and hand. (His own
body, like his beliefs, is
hidden behind the usual
trench coat.) It's enough
to take in the books, the bed,
scarves and scribbled notes,
a large ashtray that he
suddenly picks up

and then to sit silently,
alone. Like the smoke
from his innumerable
cigarettes, facts hover
in a probable fog.

What they all call

the science of deduction

comes down to one simple rule:

the body is the sole truth.

Beginning with the morning

silhouette, he moves on

to shadows burned into

the streets of destroyed

cities. Whole beings have been

reduced to light in a hideous

reversal: matter made thought.

The murdered soul wanders

nowhere, instead is trapped

in a chalk shape. He's sure

that if he put an ear to cold

concrete, he'd hear someone

wailing to be let out, like

the princess in the Chinese

myth of echo, who fell

into a vat of molten bronze

and was cast as a bell.

So the case (what a word
for that jangling mass
of brutality and doubt)
will be stubbornly put
through its paces
until the terrible
unmaking is unmasked.
As thought once more
becomes matter, the body
can be brought alarmingly
to life: this is the mystery.
Manners and money, the love
borne for another, must be
reinvented from that solitary
bit of flesh. As if eyeing it
up and down, he moves from
the shell of the victim to
the fierce pulse of survival.
For the living are infected
by oblivion, always on
the brink of falling into its

heady company. Whoever did it
will, in time, be seduced,
alone, unable to bear it
now that the dead have left
their inescapable, empty mark.

Virgin in the South

Bright juice at the corners of her mouth,
my friend in the Spanish train
smiled behind the globe
of a large apricot she nibbled.
She turned away from the window,
from the stunned countryside with its
trail of vineyards, desiccated and hopeful.
All the fruit came as a surprise;
the pulpy blood oranges in our bags
were gorgeous and close to decay,
already rotting before their prime.
The baked white soil, we thought,
had rushed them past ripening.

As we stripped for bed in our hotel
I watched her ignore the astonishing
green patterns on her underwear
that licked at her body like snakes.
Outside the Madrid fountains roared and spat,
and on the wall we found a print
of a Flemish Madonna:

a pale, imperturbable girl in red

sat ruling a room with her eyes half-closed.

Elaborate carpet, bed, firescreen

and curtain, the boxed folds of her gown

were still pregnant with intelligence

of that light pausing at the window.

The crucial child in her lap played quietly

at the center of the world. This was peace,

urging nothing, reflected only by

the glimmer, vermilion and soft gold,

of pomegranates lying asleep on the sill.

Last Seen in Jerusalem

There was hardly any mail: one postcard
with an aerial view of Corfu
and a short letter, carefully typed.
It read like the worst of those bad dramas,
a story of lust and rancor
in the holy city, a quick bilingual wedding,
and the arrival of your first male child.
After the quarrel, wife and baby left
for a country as far off as possible.

Fragments are always lost in traveling:
the book left in an airport, a trinket,
a child. The motes of your matter
fly over the wide world as you move on
and then they settle, deep within new streets,
new languages. You can beget and lose
anything over there, until your descendants
are hidden in the texture of nations.

At large, or at home, you must be parent

to a dim facsimile of childhood, while

the vanished son grows up with a gap

in his small memory. This is how to do it.

Wear your fatherhood like elaborate armor,

glittering with invented colors

like all the postcards you won't send him,

souvenirs of exotic America.

"Sur le Pont d'Avignon"

The small child suddenly in France began
to invent memory and ice: she toiled
up the frosted, incredible hill
behind a supposed parent, not seeing
the foreign city below, felled by snow.
This was Avignon, she was told, just now
finding herself where the white bridge was
forged into darkness, on a wooden bridge,
in silence. It was as tiny as she,
pale against the black bit of pond beneath
that scarcely rippled. And there were white swans
emerging from the thickets. Their red feet,
confused and living rudders, guided them,
gliding under them. They were her first swans.

In school she learned the old French dancing game.
There were so many others; all these feet
seemed to shatter the formal surface of
bowing, curtseying, and the polished floor.
One of the unusual words they sang
was "Avignon," cold, familiar, this time

with something missing as they clapped their hands
and circled like skaters, or like half-grown
foolish birds. She slowly moved her bent head,
ruffling up her skirt to supply the swans.

The chilly American woman stood
by the French windows, gazing and grieving
at the slick shine of ice-fields. The diamond-
hard ground had sprung from her infant footsteps
simply, like the easy clarity of
black water in winter, the transparent
eye of the early frost. Children on foreign
voyages never dream of the next thing:
memory froze over the swans.

Incognito

Once I threw a torn dress out a porthole:
it flapped for an outraged second and flew
down to be eaten by the Atlantic.
By now its frail pink gingham has become
fish scale, fish eye. The years and the sea-slime
made their move: and this is evolution.

Setting out in the Fifth Avenue glitter
—as the sunlit breeze glides over us all—
I metamorphose into a tourist.
This could be Paris, London, Amsterdam,
any cool northern capital that chills
in July. A reflection, mine, is stuck
in the window of an elegant shop:
dark glasses, magenta lipstick, the face
in transit, misshapen with despair. I,
caught behind this expensive scrim, am small
as a well-loved object lost in water.

Accidents

Smack in the white middle of December
I felt the new car, gray and bulbous
and glossy as a seal, spin on the ice
and ram its luxurious nose into a rail.
Straight ahead, a screen of birches parted
to reveal the cunning sparkle of the river
or maybe, I imagined, shards of glass.
Nothing broke this time. And like the stiff
enduring snow sealing up the valley,
there glowed in the sunless morning an expanse
of minutes, enough of them to keep me guessing
how it might have ended, what other life
might have monitored them.

                              Better, though,
not to think of an ending, but a shifting:
being kicked and shaken into wakefulness
with the pitching anxieties of earthquakes.
Which is ground, which is sky? How different
must I be? Is this what survival means?
One week later, you had your turn. Breaking

an actual wrist and rib in a collision
just north of here, you must have sat and shivered
with the same bad wind, the same good questions.

It's the nature of ice to be darkly honest.
It flashes—white, then black—with the welcoming
half-truth of mirrors, just as smooth and greedy
for our touch, ready to harden the world
against us when we try slipping through.
Each face will end up staring at itself,
each traveler veers off the sleepy path
and runs into the iron-hard persistence
of what's still out there.

That percussive instant
might be the double accident of our births,
the merest shrug of time and space apart,
together marking up this countryside
under the intrepid sign of the Ram. Today
let our anniversary be smitten

with a little fear and knowledge, just as the cars

and pale New England roads are mauled and dirtied.

Icy mud spatters the crunched metal

in a revelation: missing us, our death

hurls us back into the tremendous weight

of living, of bodies that can move and hurt.

The supple community of flesh and bone

is renewing itself with every shock—you'll hear

my heart speed up again—as we come skidding

into the world with a gasp, a yell, a crash.

Telling Tales

In real life, as in a story, something
must happen. That is just the trouble.
        —C. S. Lewis

The new myth remains unfinished:
a cheerful old visionary, worn out at
      last, abandoned his warped legend
without the grace of resolution, the joke
      snapped in mid-sentence. *The fair-haired*
king, victorious and far too youthful, strides
      through ruined Troy and finds Helen
old, faded, a mock of the surrounding wreck.
      What was it all for? he wonders
even as the humor, like the phrase of his
      question, is severed by pain. When
we read it aloud in the old summerhouse
      I tried to finish properly,
hoping that the low cadence of a voice would
      make up for Menelaus's loss.
We asked each other what exactly happened
      to the lady—too much sun and
smoked eels, perhaps; for the same Asian languor

hung in the noon beyond the pale
lattice-work where we sat without true movement
of thought, feeling day extend to
evening, strung along a continuous gold
shadow. The stirring into life
of tiny flies brought a sense of some darkness,
and still the king's confusion kept
us from creeping back out to the dim breezes.

I knew ("Was it all for nothing?")
how his question fell with a clatter between
us—just as he dropped his dead shield
when first confronted with the ravaged Helen—
was there a true cause for battle?
And when our towering bond crumbled into
a casual, easy rhythm,
the decade of flames and mingled strategies
(for meetings were careful attacks
and memories, sieges) dissolved in a mist.
I was caught with yellow head bent,

an old weapon hanging useless by my side,

    bland and silent, yet unaware

of the incoming tide near the great bay past

    the hills, where all of a sudden

a thousand ships vanished into the deep air.

Pillar of Salt

"This is Mars," we both say at the same
moment, opening our eyes. And yet
the waste land surrounding us is only
the gray area between motel and diner,
miles from where we usually think we are.
All night we slept in the car, not moving,
our bodies conforming to the bucket seats
like temple sculptures crushed by pediments,
or skeletons curled up in shallow graves.

The rain lies half-congealed on the road,
smothering in oil, and seems as cold
and horribly palpable as mercury.
We avoid the silver puddles as we hunt
for clocks and breakfast. In the atomic-age
blue light of the diner I keep noticing
drops of your sweat, or of incipient tears;
they look blue too, as if frozen and stained
with the nasty clarity of chemical dye.
Your face is furrowed and glistening with well-
traveled patterns, with farewells, with every

harsh distance you can imagine. "Don't look back,"
I try to say, but your cold-water gaze
is still fixed on the fatal spectacle
of where we came from. Having molded us,
it wears us down to nothing, just as years
wasted lying motionless in bed
will dissolve the bones to memorable air.

Enthralled, you sit by the window. And outside
our tiny car is squatting in the lot,
pointed towards the shore. It's clean and stubborn,
like the first sunlight forcing itself past
another world to this one, hot on your back,
urging the dumb slab of your body forward.

Central Park

One November on a nervous amble
in the chilly dusk, we stop, turn, and fall.
The corresponding flurry of dry leaves
sweeps over us, spreadeagled as we are,
drenched in the early attitudes of lovers.
Leaves alone inhabit the charged space
between us, hint and crackle underneath,
behind, around, creeping into an ear
(dangerously), across the refusing
crook of arm and sluggish knee, against
brow and eyelid and the sweat, resting there.
Lips left bare for motion or meeting, we
will stir at the chosen moment and reach
for newer terrain under all these clothes.
When our backs arch and stiffen and shudder
we will shake off the ministering leaves,
and as if in agreement with each other
our bodies will mash the life out of them.

You, Me and the Thing

Glimpsed through the half-open curtain,
we seem to be content as we are: my chair,
your cigarettes, the remains of dinner.
Or perhaps there are no curtains, and this is
the night for driving: we kiss and converse
and rub our knees on the black dashboard.
Then suddenly the air grows thick, peculiar,
and we hear the telltale scrape of branches
across the windshield—here it is! The Thing!
My scream is dark and shiny with lipstick
as the Chevy groans and something lumbers up
through the midnight wood. It throws you down
and bashes the handsome panic from your face.
It carries me off in a faint, slip rustling,
tits pushing up like turrets gone askew
in a hurricane. We're doomed to rehearse this scene
endlessly till one of us gives up.
Armored, tendriled, glittering and fanged,
crude alien or elaborate Jabberwock,
it still oozes and emanates nearby.

Glimpsed through the half-shaded window

while cruising at thirty thousand feet

rests a bulging cloud shaped like a tortoise,

like the great tortoise which is the world.

It's easily mounted on the fleecy mist.

It discloses, briefly, the delicious order

of the roads, laid out across the desert

like marks of the thinnest bearable brush.

I can see this Leviathan expand

over the tilted wing, moving this way.

I'm writing you a brave letter.

As a burst of turbulence rattles the seats

I lean back, eyelids trembling, pen at a loss

over the page. I won't try description

or memory. Both of us will only yield

to every day that gathers up and forms

our very own creature, materialized again

from the dreamy white menagerie of the sky.

The Silhouette

With coldness, with winter's tightening grip
comes the silence that should be just quiet.
You also learn about a deadly weight
pressing on your insides, as if driven
there by the soft heavy snowfalls. Above
and outside (the real outside), surfaces
of ground, bark and skin ripple sluggishly,
pushing against cold. But in the sleep of
surroundings, urges of things are pressed back
in. We moved along—walking was too brisk,
too definite—muffled in scarves and in
the numbness of an overlong winter
arising early in the choking year.

It was night, or perhaps exhausted day,
but the thumbnail moon's implied disk showed up
all the same. I thought it might be part of
the scenery—cold's landscape never shifts.
Our favorite shapes of houses looked more
like eroded mountains, and we could see

some towers reach up in angular shock.
It might have been the building we lived in.

When energy arises from nothing,
from its own lack, it dies on the first wind.
My initial sweep of vigor at the
idea of us as companions here
was cut short as it left my fingertips,
not even hovering between us for a
moment. Instead, we devoted ourselves
to the distant trees, slim reminders of
something outside and beyond our slow steps
taking root in the drifts. And I thought of
my fingertips once again, tracing them
against the snow; they seemed stuck fast to it
with the congealing air. In winter, hands
are pale, delicate and emerging things.

The effort comes then in looking around
yourself: I braced, turned and saw eyes weakened
like glass left buried in the dull, raw soil.
There was no being in the bent head next
to mine but third person, always removed
from doing and having done, always off
at the edge of statement, of direction.
This presence was the case and not the case.

When the snow fell, we could show no concern
for its light attentions. By this time we
were like two channels of ice, two columns
forced into complement by being paired.
The voice projected, the hand in gentle
counterpoint with mine, even the breath seen
echoed in fog denied a you or me
or any us. There was only a this:
the easy, simulated warmth of this
including all the world, simple presence,
two moving in moonlight, this cloud, this cold.

Views of the Studio

To the radio's hiss
the man and his black-muzzled dog are dancing;
she darts with loving tenacity at
each shuffle, each swing of the hip.
His feet dot the floor, in white socks,
like those pale aberrations of paint
living in his canvases.

There, by the remaining daylight,
still lifes are cooling.

On the table sits the day's arrangement:
apple, chipped bowl, two bottles.
What seems an intention may be just resting.
(Remember, even the big dog can be caught
easily in ink, her thoughtful haunches spread.)

Round and noble in light's casual slope,
things bloom at the accident of a glance.

They lie amassed by the bed at midnight
or touched by a movie's meandering eye.

Nightfall slips into its soft context:
man and capering dog, table
against the murky floor. Already
their outlines grow uneasy in the shade,
and echoing through the wall for a
unifying yellow pang
—lemon peel at the frame's edge—
is the gutstring wail of a child.

Ogata Kōrin
on His Field of Irises

Kyoto, c. 1701

Neither you nor I would imagine gardens
       like this, but my tacit brush
       sees differently. On the
folding screen that will invent a fresh young room
       with the stern economy
       of a knife, there arises
a company of irises and sweeping
       blades of leaf. They explode from
       gold ground (not earth but ether,
that sumptuous nothingness which the flat world
       so disrupts) as if growing
       miraculously from sand.
Descending in a skittish diagonal
       they stumble a bit, but then
       it's you who must be stumbling
in this burning gold envelope of summer.
       Your head lolls along with the
       plushy tip of each flower
as if you had laced their scent with your *sake*.

Now we both know they might be

calligraphy after all,

delicious ideograms in just two styles

of purple, and the poem

encoded in their nodding

petals will speak no louder than a whisper.

Three homesick gentlemen stopped

to weep at the eight-fold bridge

overgrown with irises. Inspired by grief,

they composed an acrostic

lament on the syllables

of iris, more a sigh than a word, really,

in pale English: to the left

all disappears off the edge

only to start again, in the following

panel, with a few opaque

stalks, like a voice rising in

gentle inquiry as it murmurs *iris.*

The garrulous right-hand screen,

though, whose chatter of blossoms

peaks and ebbs as they scallop across the air

with the eager precision

of architectural bays,

will only answer with *kakitsubata:*

the drawn-out stutter of sobs

like those of the courtiers,

choking with sentiment and poetizing,

who cried until their lunch of

dried rice was dampened with tears.

I paint, naturally, for money. What can

summon all this eloquent

growth as urgently as gain?

On the other hand, you might say that I paint

money itself, that the gold

medium where nature springs

is every coin ever coveted, now ground

to powder and sprinkled on

the waiting screen, now warming

and at last melting happily in the sun.

Wealth, like a rare essence, can

flower from the minimal.

Soothing the rich, my resonant irises
are still richer themselves: for
look how simply they bestow
a lush nostalgia on the chamber where you
make love, make tea, give or take
counsel! Real privilege is
what we mean by art, where the satisfaction
you seek effortlessly bears
you up with the elegant
starkness of purple, green, gold. Each unadorned
leaf startles with intent, like
a woman's bright wrist and knee
parting her kimono as she leans forward
to hand me a new iris
of my own. Tearing apart
the petals I observe once more how painting
reduces truth. What we make
from nothing need only be
enough for recognition: the audacious
colors conceived on precious

metal, no eight-fold bridge, no

time, place, tears. These are already among your

luxurious possessions

which, in the old days, were quite

understood—and how I'd welcome a signal

from the lean past in these hot,

bedizened days, from what our

weak emperors have lost! Here, only here, is

the flower of that court, with

its pleasure and clarity

and with its sorrowing gentlemen poets,

a material world of

things left glowingly unsaid.

The Candid Shot

In a photograph, it's been said before,
all fact becomes opinion. But just look
at these two! Being so much themselves
has frozen them into a polychromed emblem
to be taken out and frowned over, later.
As soon as the camera went up he stiffened,
she pulled her coat closer, and now here
she is, taut and talkative, coffee cup
steadied on a tanned knee. He looks over
(dark, hunched) with a smile pulled into place
by something easily missed—habit? Regret?
And what about the quiver around the mouth,
or the loathing purring in the heavy throat?
Even with a magnifying glass it's hard
to map the movement of that sidelong glance:
the eyes slide painfully to the right, knowing
what it is they'll rest upon, what it is
that wrenches them around in their bloody beds.

The background wall dissolves to a dim orange
as fast film annihilates every outline.

There, just visible in that momentous
failure of definition, is the signal
for great buildings to totter and crash down
when the earth slides right out from under them,
or to blow stupidly apart in the endless
versions of war that shock us awake, often.
Fear settles like smoke in the darkened room,
though dials and digitals keep quietly winking,
and the whirr of the illuminated fishtank
whispers your name. For all the mechanisms
you gather to yourself like limbs, like folds
of the quilt, the camera out there offers
no escape; the sunlit world takes aim.

The Auto-Architect

Looking at a building, they never
imagine the body of the man who
built it. Yes, there exists a genius
of the edifice, ethereal and huge:
in secret, his phantom hands descend
to touch the cornices and roof as fondly
as he had touched the tiny white model,
as sadly as Pygmalion in love.
But for the viewers there is only
blasted rock and their smallness, fixing them
like the rough statues they seem to see.

I found you, artisan, in a struggle
with all of air and substance to carve
your own odd hollow, your own solution.
Just like the old builders who made their blood
mortar, buried in their cornerstones,
you cast yourself in a perfect niche,
wanting to be no less than stone itself.
First you appeared as flesh—a naked man
framed in rock, tinted and shivering—
then chilled with time into the stuff of myth.

Now monochromed, beyond movement, you stand
for the tremors beneath the final surface:
the sudden harsh slip of rock against rock,
the poor hot basalt that suffers so
gloriously under the earth's weight just as
a body in bed shifts under its other.
In cold exquisite silence, your mouth
is stuffed shut by the deep kiss of marble,
while marble pinions your limbs in its
hungry gray fabric. Your blank eyes
are lit by some mirrored hall within;
nakedness is fraught with geometry.
In the endless museum of structures
that fills our perilous space, I find
myself confronted by this hidden statue.
I have to shelter my gaze from you,
artful paradigm, as you let the stone
surround you—skin, robe, cathedral,
utterance—the vault of definition.

Magnificat

When the choir begins its bitter ascent
each interval pulls me towards you.
The notes grow keener and tighter
up to the last point in the scale
from which our voices fall
like scraps of paper fluttering
to the ground, or hang pure
like motes in the sunbeam
piercing the cathedral window.

This time I understand
the struggle of counterpoint:
the higher parts, yours and mine,
are fighting like angry, proud children,
splendid in their difference.
It can only be this refusal of union
that has broken us up into Bach.
For us a fugue is one in a series
of impassioned arguments: we all keep
protesting, from bass to soprano,
with ever louder, ever more

familiar rhetoric. Listen:

we feel this way, and that way,

and thus, and, finally, completely.

This is how to mourn, to cheer, and

of course to love, which is simple

and always expected as we move,

hesitating, into our cadence.

As our voices flirt and bicker,

boldly overlapping or dancing apart,

the great walls hang back as witnesses.

In this devout, ambitious building

every stone soaks up the noise of praise

like water; it swells with the nourishment

or splashes it back in an answering

shout of laughter. Catching a quick

breath, I wait for everything to

quake and crumble with our disagreements.

The cathedral itself might be ripped

in two volatile parts just like

your treble, my descant. Keep singing,

and watch the baroque angels in the loft,

both of them, holding their slim trumpets

a perpetual few inches from their lips.

Watch them now as they start to

shift on their plaster clouds and

kick at their draperies with

restless, invisible feet. Keep singing.

Agalma

Marble, pink and weathered, over
a ton of it, has taken form
this time in the museum storehouse
as a Greek kouros: huge warrior
or athlete, perhaps god, sheathed
in nakedness and a shining smile.
He lies—enormous—and looks up
as if in amused sufferance
at being examined by the students.
Wearing surgical gloves,
they stroke the iliac ridge
or the hillocks of the abdomen,
and frown over unhelpful photographs.
(He is in several pieces, all huge.)
They turn over the forearm
to expose, in its recent break,
the chunky white crystals
glittering joyfully like new snow.
They trace the sweep of the thighs,
of the cheekbones, and the hair
that resembles ropes of fat pearls
clinging to his secret back.

Muscled and feminine thing, he kept

his clenched fists at his sides

for always, in the grave

or sanctuary where he stood

while the smile reassured, defied.

Now flattened by history, the votive

is oddly horizontal, with his

small neat sex jutting outward

to affirm all that's animate.

Now the striding left leg,

marvelous holy engine of life,

aims a reactive kick at the sky.

He might shift on his Styrofoam bed,

inviting a tumble among his broken limbs:

an arm, a foot, a decorative knee

lie scattered around him like pillows.

The basement is as silent

as a dissecting theater—here

they all set their teeth against

the chill and color of time gone.

But this is no cadaver. The body
unearthed has always been alive,
just as the translucent marble
whose glow was lulled into dust
by layers of dumb greenery
has never stopped breathing. (A fly
settling on the comfortable rock lips
darts away at once, maybe sensing
how easily they could curl and part.)
And if he does move, it will simply be
out of obedience to his builder.
The various pieces of him
will disseminate his beauty
as a candid offering
called *agalma*, delight,
as stone is blessed with shape.

Laying aside a heavy text,
you lean over and touch him.
You've come to know each vein and bone

acknowledged in the wrought surface
and speak their names without thinking,
like the names of your children.
Handling every human lump as you must,
you'll find your parts mirroring his own
and in turn, elbow and giant thumb
may answer your exploring pressure.
Meeting is a magnificent handshake
as the great white archaic grasp,
long since severed at the wrist,
expands from your small worn paw.

Best, while working, to close your eyes
and insist on the primacy of touch,
as inquisitive and abrupt
as a boy's when surrounded
by fragments of clamorous nudity,
stealing a feel in the antiquities room.
Hands, your hands, are always caught
by the befuddlement of sculpture.

63

Traversing neck and shoulder,

bit by bit, like dull insects,

they halt with indecision:

skin or stone? Chisel marks

or fresh wisps of hair?

Like bard and oracle, be blind.

What's truly living in a living shape

rises, flutters, and persuades,

spelling out its message

in the swell of breast and inner arm

that forever moves you like marble.

Back in the Twilight Zone

for David Leavitt

In the television's pale square of light
there stretches a paler desert, small town
skirted by the loneliest of mountains,
or the hot surface of an asteroid.
Wherever it is, it's summer, always
and ever after, flooding this landscape
of fear with its bright, banal deception.
Soon a hapless man will wander into
the frame and try to feel at home, looking
for a sign, a telephone pole, footprints.
Perhaps this is the world after the bomb
and he the final astronaut, alone
and uncomprehending; in any case
those who constantly watch him will know first.

In the evening grasses of New England
a boy sits upright and recognizes
traffic, shouts, and churchbells. He remembers
being driven through the desert, frightened

even by the serene forks of cactus

that guarded the immense family car.

For there was death in the open, not caught

for a crazy instant in the dread eyes

of buffalo skulls (as a camera

would have it), but glaring eternally,

just as day frowns on a parched asteroid.

He dreamed he found a pair of glasses there

with hypnotic powers. They were throwing

gleams on the already gleaming dust, like

sunlight piercing a television screen

with fiercer reflection.

In a small hot lens every place becomes

empty of events. The boy knows of this

from staring at deserts on the late show,

where the known horizon disappears

in a blinding concavity of sky.

He takes off his own innocent glasses:

his eyes are edged with mauve shadows, as if

bruised by what they saw out there in the sand,

what lost aliens and astronauts saw.

And like the damp grass clinging to his skin,

like the first prickle of disease, he feels

a sudden enormous silence switch on

that can only mean someone is watching.

You Are Here

When you plan to go anywhere
this is how things appear
in the great urban diagrams:
a dim fluorescent arrow trembles at
an impossible space, your space
and starting point. Now
you're guided through mazes
that could be streets, hallways, aisles,
whatever lines will pull you
into the cool grid of the known.

Weary from rebellious zigzags
over the continent, you found
your way along the sky's corridor
and halted, perfectly, in a corner
of my apartment. The floor's edges
meet seamlessly and forever
in the back bedroom. There
you lie jetlagged and asleep,
tucked away at this intersection

of white wall and ceiling

that keeps you from getting lost.

Not far off, I'm going nowhere

but into the kitchen; and

over the echo of pot and kettle

as I make coffee, I can hear

the foreign dust from your body

settling, settling.

The Wanderer's Journal

The man who walked through Europe one winter,

bidden there by some private agony,

has published a diary of his trek.

The first time I left home alone, it was in

a dark hotel that I sat sleepless,

reading this romance of isolation.

Setting out in a cruel German blizzard,

he headed west: children from the small towns

were frightened of his wet, contorted face;

young girls in peasant costume looked away

and blushed.

Only the man with boots, beard and compass

can become a wanderer. He alone

carves out a path through the frozen birch

ahead of him, as the telegraph wires

sweep the roads with a grace determined

to flee the clutch of ice. His wife is left

to work on her soups and her paragraphs.

He calls her often, from pay telephones

where his quick tears congeal and stick fiercely,

then breaks into abandoned summer homes
to bandage his feet.

He rests at an inn and orders hot food.
Painted on his plate are a rural church
and two farm women with their backs to him,
their skirts stiffened like a wall. And he writes
I stare for a while, then I disappear
with these women into the white picture,
into that church. Now I try vanishing
into the book lost on my lap. I see
that it lies only one step beyond
the warmth of a room anywhere over
the earth. And there the man waits and writes
before heading again into the mist
and thunder from the gray mountains, into
an emptiness that shouts from the valley,
astonishing him with its wide embrace.

The Soccer Game outside Munich

The Regelbach Kickers win their last game.
Most of them might be cousins: postman, cop,
teacher, baker, artisan, and of course
the film director, who rips off his thin
jersey, flings it at the devouring clouds
and scores a goal. All the bearded players,
their knees silver and their farmers' brown curls
dancing in the drizzle, cry something and
skid over the ancestral flats of mud.
The German eludes us. So we shiver
on a wet bench made by the woodcarver
(the quickest player here), and heed the rain
as it levels natives and visitors
to grass or mud, sliding past the far trees
like a perpetual hiss of applause.

But the rain will grow heavy and plaintive
and will draw us downward, refusing us
more bright glimpses of the brown men playing.
At the final goal it will drown the cheers

burying themselves in its new furrows;

will drown the town, the city, the homeland

lying just a shout and a kick away.

Via Faenza

One of them, groping naked in the dust
of a dark apartment somewhere in the city,
brushes by things her eyes distort in sleep:
wardrobe, easel, chair, she learns their history
from touching them, like following a map
that marks each bend and shallow of a river.

Past the black window she can hear the river
flowing south. Narrow, tawny with dust,
it's as hard to navigate as any map
of streets and piazzas in this famous city
with its obstacle course of monuments, its history.
The traces are endless—one could go to sleep

counting statues. The other one, asleep,
lies on the bed like one of those stone river-
gods, a sprawled figure out of ancient history:
stilled heavy genitals, beard dripping dust,
hands massive enough to crush a city,
and veins on the legs tracing their marble map.

She crouches down, discovering the map
that fell from the table as he fell asleep.
Between the lines that imitate the city
are spaces for flecks or blue smears on the river,
the signs of foreigners beating down the dust.
Each is a chip or fraction with no history,

solemnly absorbing all the history
of the present place, as if the usual map
could point to tragedy hidden in the dust.
Here's tyranny, war, and then the flood, when sleep
was troubled deep inside the feverish river
that moaned, stirred, and rolled over on its city.

And under its briny layers the stained city
pulses the way he breathes, flowing past history,
past histrionic, smoother than a river.
As she nears the wall its cracks become a map
that rises from the bed to plot their sleep.
Slid in the sheets, her feet are filmed with dust

like travel dust or silt from the aging river.

The city puts an evening on the map:

one sleeps, one doesn't. The rest is always history.

The Mourner

Descending, the narrow view aft of the wing
reveals nothing but a few lights and clouds—
or at least those passages of obscurity
you hope are only clouds, rather than lapses
in memory or in creation itself.
They blot the shining water, bridge and suburb
like black patches of paint smeared crossly
over an earlier version of the world.
Blind, you give yourself to the express trains.

As you spin awake in the sweaty guest bed
you claw at the mattress, kneading the pillow
into a small apologetic mass
to grab from behind and throttle with your knees.
The jaws of the bereft beast City
are advancing just beyond the summer screens.
Enraged, you snap back, reflecting for a second
its myriad lit windows in your bared teeth.

Someone at the other end of town
is dying, and the streets are hot with cracks.

Huge ziggurats downtown need just that final

intake of breath to heave and split and blaze.

As brief as coughs, the flames are splattered up

and annihilated in the smudgy sky.

You're losing. Shutting your eyes, you recognize

the echoing earth's moans and creaks, down low

in the abysses of the avenues

like tired machinery rusting to a stop,

only a shrinking mile from where you lie.

Route 280

In this valley lies
the heart of science fiction country:
some future amphitheater of terror
where the hills make way, soundlessly,
for the thrust of alien metal.

Any arrival could hide over the bland horizon
while we talk in the car.
Your awkward white hand gropes the gearshift
as you ponder, mutter, and heeding, smile back.

The freeway lights greet us far ahead,
set in the calm slope
like gemstones on a bit of proffered skin.

Still, when we reach them
can never be very important. You and I
will always be absent from
our great moments—one of the stars

suddenly plunging down, a peerless

new presence startling us into tears,

that first inkling of another body

easing its way in.

When we roll on the yielding road

we notice nothing. Earth shifts knowingly

with our weight, taking its cue from

the black sky, accepting us

for the strangers we clearly are.

Difficult Movie

Reflected horribly in the grand piano,

the sky is offered up as your accompanist.

You pick out a melody with one hand,

sweating and waiting, while

the apartment stays unremittingly gray.

When she walks in through the half-open door

(an identical door can be glimpsed behind),

she seems to bring color with her.

Now you begin the dialogue of murmured threats

and non sequiturs, and stare each other down.

The blinds throw satisfying stripes along a wall,

movements of sunlight litter the carpet,

and everywhere are the sweet gleams of

her earrings, your shared wineglass, a gun.

As you fall to kissing, twisting damply

in your sweaters, your own face

is smeared in a rictus of fear:

you're doomed if she speaks your name.

Yet your stalking and embracing change nothing.

Even at the odd instant she disappears

no wave or shiver mars the peace of walls.
The place is as unremarkable as glass,
a fishbowl revealing the flicker
of every bright fin, but itself
solid and motionless,
boring, and so easy to destroy.

You're in the middle of your walk
and your fingers are skating
on the granite sides of buildings.
The gun reposes against your skin, only
inches from the heart, and as you touch them,
the things of the world will touch you back.
Wordless and huge, desire animates every
point in the stone city's air, as if
the strip of sidewalk beneath you
needed your step to go on being there.

Sunburn

for Muriel Wolf

Summer's end: at the rooftop barbecue
the supple tar bakes naked
as we would like to, swallowing rum
and twitching in the sun.
Surrounding buildings are poised quietly
like desert predators at a watering place.
Drunk, unprotected, we rashly expose
ourselves to the warmth of attention,
ignited in us, it seems,
by each stinging morsel we eat
(cardamom, lime juice, cayenne).
Recognition strikes our skin
like an unseen, harmful ray.

It gets darker: the thinning
of this beneficent September air
sets our teeth chattering, a
surprise that banishes all thoughts of heat.
Know that responsibility is at its cold heart,

that tending our new burns,

testing their reddened borders,

is a way of survival.

My dear, be careful.

We should watch for that sly moment

when the temperature drops, when faces die,

when our last dish of ice cream

(mostly blueberry)

describes the color of the autumn sky.

In the Museum

Now, finally, we come to Vincent's wheatfields,
each one a window that pierces the gallery,
opening on a dense, fevered landscape
of impulse. Leaves and branches, narrow paths
and clumps of chimneys in the vigorous distance
ruffle as paper does when it starts to burn.
That thick stroke, here in life-giving yellow,
there in blue, parodies a caress
that pulls back even as it agitates
and arouses. The moment it licks the canvas
it darts up fearfully against the wall,
snarling like ivy. So the sad man twists
his epileptic shape into his craft,
planting a riot of want in God's garden.

Imagine a museum without art,
an impossible rotunda of granite glowing
bare and roseate under the tungsten beam.
Expertly designed for show and tell,
its archways and erotic surfaces
endlessly repeat around the night-
filled space. Making your way along each curve

of the charmed corridor, you would reach out
to feel the smoothness breathe under your hand,
just as your sharp heels, clacking smartly,
would play the music you were waiting for.

At closing time all the exits look
suspiciously alike. And only then
can our figures be cunningly discerned
in the undulating forest of men and women
retreating or easing forward for better views.
We smile at one another like paintings.
In this echoing and mutable grove
all our remembered softness, heft and scent
flicker the way the earliest stars flicker
behind the trees. We rouse ourselves to reach
or gesture, sculpting in the air, rhyming
and golden like heraldic animals.
We are no less than this. The pictures leap
in their frames while their insistent yellow
stirs us to the laughter of great beasts,
rampant and absolute as the lights go down.